LADY LIBERTY
SYMBOL OF A NATION

Retold by
KATE SHOUP

Illustrated by
JOEL GENNARI

Cavendish
Square
New York

PEOPLE ALL OVER THE WORLD KNOW ABOUT LADY Liberty. Lady Liberty is the personification of America. She is a character who stands for the United States of America. She also stands for the ideas of liberty and freedom.

When most people think of Lady Liberty, they think of the Statue of Liberty. France gave the Statue of Liberty to America in the late 1800s. It was built by Frédéric Auguste Bartholdi and Gustave Eiffel. Bartholdi and Eiffel wanted to build the statue to celebrate America's one hundredth birthday in 1876. However, they did not finish the statue until ten years later.

The Statue of Liberty sits on a small island in New York Harbor. She greets the ships coming in. When immigrants moved here from other countries, the statue was often the first thing they saw. Immigrants were people who left their home countries to start a new life in another country.

An ancient statue called the Colossus of Rhodes inspired the Statue of Liberty. The Colossus of Rhodes was built in Greece in 280 BCE. It was 108 feet (33 meters) high. The Statue of Liberty is three times that size. It stands 305 feet 6 inches (93 m) tall. (This includes her pedestal.) That's as tall as a twenty-two-story building! Her index finger alone is 8 feet (2.4 m) long and her waist is 35 feet (10.7 m) around. The Statue of Liberty weighs 450,000 pounds (204.1 metric tons).

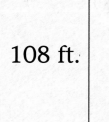

108 ft.

305 ft.

The statue is made of copper. Copper is a brown color. Over time, the copper changes to a greenish color. The Statue of Liberty looks green today because it is very old. The statue shows a woman wearing a long robe called a toga and a crown. The crown has seven points. These points stand for Earth's seven continents and seven seas.

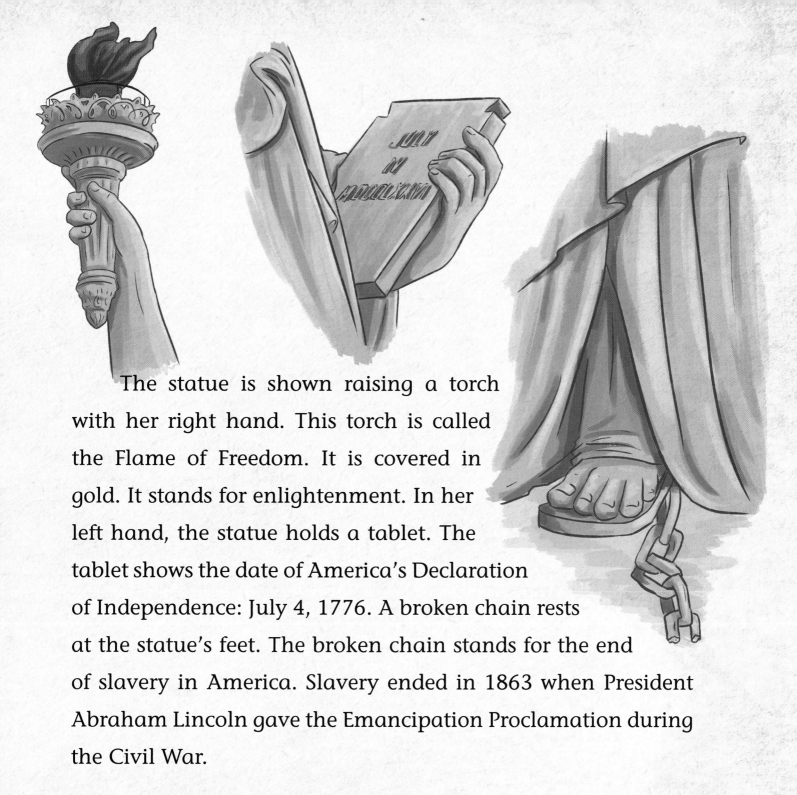

The statue is shown raising a torch with her right hand. This torch is called the Flame of Freedom. It is covered in gold. It stands for enlightenment. In her left hand, the statue holds a tablet. The tablet shows the date of America's Declaration of Independence: July 4, 1776. A broken chain rests at the statue's feet. The broken chain stands for the end of slavery in America. Slavery ended in 1863 when President Abraham Lincoln gave the Emancipation Proclamation during the Civil War.

8

Today the Statue of Liberty is the most famous image of Lady Liberty in America. But she is not the only one. Before the Statue of Liberty, there was another statue of Lady Liberty in the United States. It is called the Statue of Freedom.

This statue was built by Thomas Crawford in 1863. It stands on top of the United States Capitol Building in Washington, DC. The statue is very shiny. It shows a woman wearing a toga. Over the toga is a blanket trimmed with fur and fringe, like those worn by Native Americans. The statue also wears a helmet. It looks like an eagle's head with feathers. The eagle is an emblem of America. The statue holds a sword in her right hand. This stands for America's military power. In her left hand, the statue holds a wreath and a shield. The wreath stands for victory in the American Revolution (1775–1783). The shield has thirteen stripes. There is one stripe for each of the original thirteen American colonies.

The idea of Lady Liberty goes back to ancient Greece and ancient Rome. The Greeks and Romans believed in many gods and goddesses. One Greek goddess was Eleutheria. Eleutheria was the goddess of liberty. Historians know very little about her. They know more about the Roman goddess Libertas. She was also a goddess of liberty. In stories, Libertas was the daughter of Roman gods Jupiter and Juno. Jupiter was king of the gods. Juno was his wife. Libertas stood for the idea of freedom—especially freedom from slavery. She also stood for the idea of a republic. A republic is a type of government that is ruled by the people.

Romans began worshipping Libertas when Rome became a republic in 509 BCE. They built buildings called temples to honor her. The most famous temple for Libertas was in Rome. It had big columns and shiny statues.

Romans also built a statue of Libertas in a part of Rome called the Roman Forum. Historians think ancient Romans visited this statue when they wanted to free their slaves.

The Romans had lots of different ideas about what Libertas looked like, what she carried, and what she wore. Usually she carried a rod called a vindicta or a pole called a liberty pole. The rod was used in ceremonies for freeing slaves. Sometimes she held an olive branch. This stood for peace. Other times she carried a cornucopia. It stood for wealth or having a lot of things. Sometimes a cat sat at her feet. The cat stood for watchfulness. Often she carried or wore a cap called a pileus. This was worn by freed slaves in ancient Rome. Usually she wore a toga, but sometimes she was naked! Today you can see different forms of Libertas on ancient Roman coins.

In 476 CE, the Roman Empire fell.
During the Middle Ages, people stopped
worshipping Roman gods and goddesses.
Instead, many people became Christians.
The temple for Libertas in Rome crumbled.
People forgot about Libertas.

That changed in the 1400s. During that time, people rediscovered Greek and Roman culture. They became interested in Greek and Roman ideas. They learned about Greek and Roman gods and goddesses.

Holland

Germany

Belgium

Switzerland

France

Czech
Republic

Austria

Hungary

Italy

In the 1600s, the country of Holland became a republic. The Dutch people chose Libertas as a symbol for their country. Soon, other countries started using Libertas as a symbol. One of these countries was the United States.

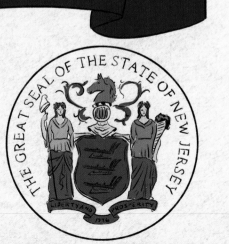

In 1776, one of America's Founding Fathers, Paul Revere, made a coin with a picture of Libertas, or Liberty, on the back. On the coin, Liberty held a liberty pole and the scales of justice. A cat sat at her feet. Around her were the words "Liberty and Virtue." This was the first of many early American coins showing the goddess Liberty. After the American Revolution, Liberty appeared on the New York State flag and on the state seal for Virginia and New Jersey.

France also used Libertas as a symbol. They called her Marianne. The name "Marianne" came from the two most popular names for girls in France during the late 1700s: Marie and Anne. To France, Marianne stood for three things: liberty, the French Revolution, and France. During World War II (1939–1945), Marianne also stood for victory against the Nazis. Like Libertas, Marianne often wears a pileus and is shown with a cat.

Marianne has appeared on many French coins and stamps. She also appears on the Great Seal of France wearing a robe and crown like the Statue of Liberty's.

21

Lady Liberty is not the only personification of America. Another famous example is a male character called Uncle Sam. Uncle Sam became popular during the early 1800s. He is still used as a symbol of America today. However, Uncle Sam doesn't stand for liberty. Instead, he stands for the US government.

Another personification of America is Columbia. Columbia is a female character. She is named after the explorer Christopher Columbus. Sometimes Columbia wears a toga. Other times she wears a dress that is red, white, and blue. Sometimes the dress has stars and stripes like the American flag. Often she wears feathers, a crown, or a cap on her head.

Columbia is not used as a symbol of America anymore. By 1900, she had been replaced by Lady Liberty—specifically the Statue of Liberty—as the main personification of America.

Today the Statue of Liberty is an American icon. The statue has appeared on many American coins. For example, twenty-five-cent coins that honor the state of New York feature the Statue of Liberty. The ten-dollar bill shows a picture of her torch.

The Statue of Liberty has also been on many American postage stamps. The US military has also used it on posters to try to get people to join.

But that's not all. You may have seen Lady Liberty or the Statue of Liberty in books or movies. In *Ghostbusters II* (1989), the statue comes to life! The statue is shown in comic books like *Wonder Woman* and *Teenage Mutant Ninja Turtles* and in video games like *Lego Marvel Super Heroes* (2013).

FIRST-CLASS

USA

Sports teams also like to use the name Liberty. The New York Liberty team in the Women's National Basketball Association is named for the statue. There is even a trick football play named after it.

Lady Liberty and the Statue of Liberty often stand for the United States in political cartoons. A political cartoon is a drawing that shows an opinion about a current event. In these cartoons, Lady Liberty might be shown laughing, crying, or even fighting. This is to show how many Americans may feel about the event.

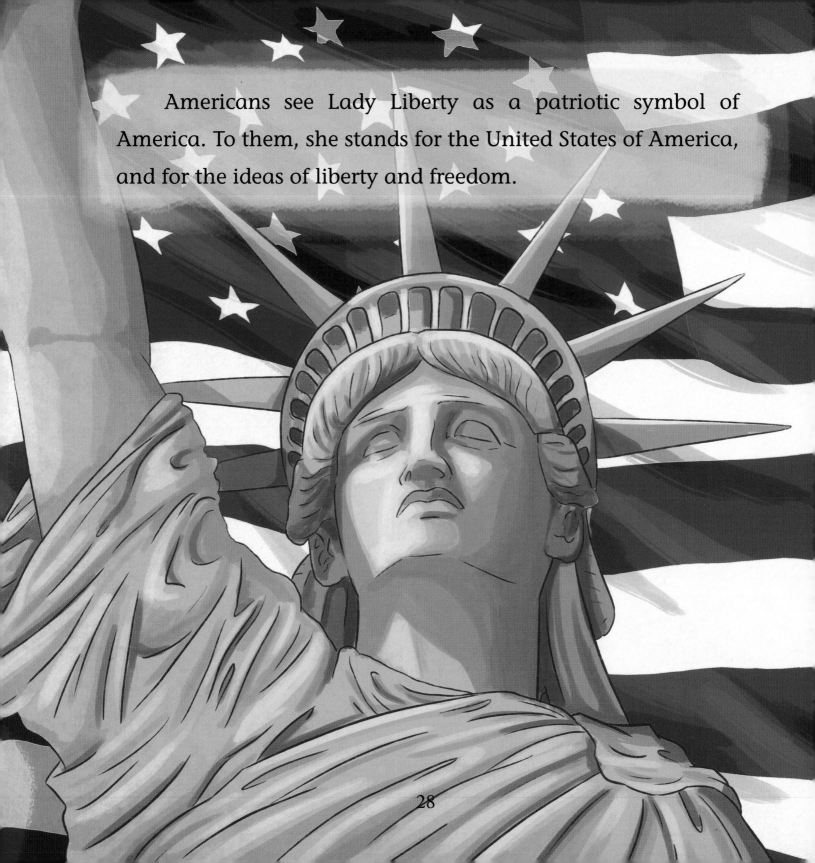

Americans see Lady Liberty as a patriotic symbol of America. To them, she stands for the United States of America, and for the ideas of liberty and freedom.

ABOUT THE LEGEND

Lady Liberty has changed over time. Thousands of years ago, she was a Greek goddess named Eleutheria. Then, around 500 BCE, she became a Roman goddess named Libertas. Romans worshipped Libertas until the fall of Rome in 476 CE. After that, Libertas was forgotten for more than a millennium. Then, in 1581, the Dutch Republic formed. The Dutch Republic chose Libertas as a symbol. Later, more countries followed. In 1776, Libertas became a symbol for the American colonies. They called her Liberty. In 1792, Libertas became a symbol for France. They called her Marianne. Today the most famous version of Lady Liberty is the Statue of Liberty in New York Harbor. She was built in 1886.

WORDS TO KNOW

cornucopia A basket shaped like a horn.

emblem A symbol.

enlightenment The gaining of knowledge and understanding.

Founding Father One of the men who helped create the United States of America.

fringe Thread, fur, or fabric that dangles from a piece of clothing or a blanket.

personification A character that represents a place or idea.

TO FIND OUT MORE

BOOKS

Eggers, Dave. *Her Right Foot.* San Francisco, CA: Chronicle Books, 2017.

Rustad, Martha. *Why Is the Statue of Liberty Green?* Our American Symbols. Minneapolis, MN: Millbrook Press, 2014.

WEBSITE

American-Historama: Statue of Liberty Facts
http://www.american-historama.org/1881-1913-maturation-era/statue-of-liberty-facts-kids.htm
Read fun facts about the Statue of Liberty on this page.

ABOUT THE AUTHOR

Kate Shoup has written more than forty books and has edited hundreds more. When not working, Shoup, an IndyCar fanatic, loves to ski, read, and ride her motorcycle. She lives in Indianapolis, Indiana, with her husband, her daughter, and their dog. To learn more about Shoup and her work, visit http://www.kateshoup.com.

ABOUT THE ILLUSTRATOR

Joel Gennari is a freelance illustrator, designer, and artist living in New York City. His breadth of work encompasses being a published children's book illustrator and cover artist, as well as having experience in concept art, graphic design, and even puppet design/creation. He is extremely comfortable working in many different mediums from digital to traditional pen and ink or watercolor, though he is probably best known for his digital comic book style. For more about him, visit his website: http://www.joelgennari.com.

Published in 2019 by Cavendish Square Publishing, LLC
243 5th Avenue, Suite 136, New York, NY 10016

Website: cavendishsq.com

This publication represents the opinions and views of the author based on his or her personal experience, knowledge, and research. The information in this book serves as a general guide only. The author and publisher have used their best efforts in preparing this book and disclaim liability rising directly or indirectly from the use and application of this book.

All websites were available and accurate when this book was sent to press.

Names: Shoup, Kate, 1972- author. | Gennari, Joel, illustrator.
Title: Lady Liberty / Kate Shoup ; illustrated by Joel Gennari.
Description: First edition. | New York : Cavendish Square, 2018. |
Series: American legends and folktales | Audience: Grades 3-5.
Identifiers: LCCN 2017048055 (print) | LCCN 2017058308 (ebook) | ISBN 9781502636874 (ebook) |
ISBN 9781502636867 (library bound) | ISBN 9781502639318 (pbk.) | ISBN 9781502636881 (6 pack)
Subjects: LCSH: Statue of Liberty (New York, N.Y.)--History--Juvenile literature. |
New York (N.Y.)--Buildings, structures, etc.--Juvenile literature.
Classification: LCC F128.64.L6 (ebook) | LCC F128.64.L6 S54 2018 (print) | DDC 974.7/1--dc23
LC record available at https://lccn.loc.gov/2017048055

Editorial Director: David McNamara
Editor: Kristen Susienka
Copy Editor: Alex Tessman
Associate Art Director: Amy Greenan
Designer: Alan Sliwinski
Illustrator: Joel Gennari
Production Coordinator: Karol Szymczuk

Printed in the United States of America